Who is Jesus?

AUTHOR:
Joy Takashi-Tanap

ILLUSTRATOR: Ayan Mansoori
CONCEPT ARTIST: Joanna Rivera

1

Little Rapha asked his mom,
"Who is Jesus, where is he from?"

2

His mommy smiled for she is glad,
"Jesus is the Son of God!"

Matthew 14:33, Mark 3:11, Luke 1:35, Luke 4:41, John 1:34, John 11:27

3

From Heaven,
he came down to Earth.
The angels sang
upon his birth!

Luke 2:8-14

The sick were healed, the poor were fed,
and he gave life upon the dead!

John 4:46-54, John 6:5-14, John 11:1-45

5

The sinners came
and he forgave.
Luke 19:1-10, John 8:1-11

He changed
their hearts,
"Jesus saves!"
John 3:16

When Pharisees saw what he did,
they had him wounded, they had him bled.

Matthew 26:47 - Matthew 27:31

They had him carry a heavy cross,
then freed a man named Barabbas.

Matthew 27:11-33

And on that cross, he's crucified.
He bore our sins and then he died.
Matthew 27:27-44, Mark 15:16-32

9

Jesus' love overcame death, so on the third day he came back to life!

Luke 24:1-12

10

He brought with him, one great reward,
salvation for everyone through Jesus Christ!

John 14:6, Ephesians 2:8-9, John 3:16, Acts 16:30-33

Eternal life awaits a man,
with God in Heaven he will find!

John 3:16, Ephesians 2:8-10, Romans 6:23, John 5:24,
Matthew 25:46, Romans 10:13, John 3:36

"So, who is Jesus?", mommy asked.
Little Rapha said at last:

13

He is my Giver,
he is my Healer,
and most of all...

Matthew 14:13-21, Luke 7:1-17

SICKNESS

Do you want to accept Jesus Christ as your Savior?
You can! Just say this prayer with me!

Dear, Lord Jesus.
Thank you for coming down
from Heaven and giving
your life for me.
Thank you for being there
every step of the way.
Thank you for the forgiveness
of my sins.

Today, I give my life to you
and accept you into my heart
as my Lord, God, and Savior.
May you remember my name
in the Book of Life.
I love you, Lord Jesus,
for you have loved me first.

In Jesus' name I pray.
Amen.

My Bible Story Guide

In a small town called Bethlehem, Joseph and Mary went but found no inn where they could rest for the night. The inn owner took heart and led them to a place where animals are kept. On that fateful evening, Jesus was born in a manger! The angels were singing, the shepherds were praising God because the Savior of the world was finally born! *Luke 2:1-16*

There were countless miracles that Jesus Christ did in the Bible. He made the crippled walk, the blind see, and the deaf hear. He also fed 5000 people with only five loaves and two fishes!

Even more amazing, he brought his dead friend Lazarus to life—four days after Lazarus was buried! See how he loves each one of us so much? *John 4:46-54, John 6:5-14, John 11:1-45*

17

My Bible Story Guide

It was supposed to be an ordinary early morning at the temple for Jesus Christ and he was ready to teach the people. Suddenly, the scribes and Pharisees brought to him a woman caught in adultery. Before, women caught in adultery were stoned to death, so the Pharisees asked Jesus Christ if the same should be done to the woman.

Jesus stood and wrote something on the ground. Then he said, "He who is without sin among you, let him throw a stone at her first."

After that, all the people judging the woman left. Because everyone knew they were also sinners. Jesus looked at the woman and said, "Neither do I condemn you; go and sin no more." *John 7:53-8:11*

18

Zacchaeus was a small tax collector. During his time, the people didn't like tax collectors. One day, Zacchaeus learned that Jesus was visiting Jericho, where he lived. He learned about how Jesus loves everyone, including tax collectors such as himself! When Jesus came, Zacchaeus could not get a good sight of the Messiah because of his short stature. So, he climbed up a sycamore tree to get a better view of Jesus. Jesus noticed Zacchaeus and talked to him! That evening, Jesus stayed at Zacchaeus' house for dinner.

The tax collector promised the Messiah that he would give half of his possessions to the poor, and if he cheated anybody, he would pay back four times the amount of what he took! *Luke 19:1-10*

My Bible Story Guide

Sometimes, people make bad decisions, just like you and me.

When Jesus stood before the governor, it was accustomed that a prisoner shall be released as the people wished. Jesus was arrested because some people didn't want to believe that God sent him as the Messiah.

Instead of choosing to release Jesus Christ, the people chose Barabbas, a notorious prisoner! However, it was the will of God for Jesus Christ to be crucified. Do you think the people chose the right decision? Why? Matthew 27

After Jesus Christ was crucified, he was laid to rest inside a tomb sealed by a huge rock.

When the women went to the tomb to visit Jesus, they found the stone rolled away! And when they entered the tomb, they did not find the body of Jesus!

Suddenly, two men in shining clothes appeared beside them and said, "Why do you look for the living among the dead? He is not here; he has risen! Remember how he told you, while he was still with you in Galilee:'The Son of Man must be delivered over to the hands of sinners, be crucified and on the third day be raised again.' " Luke 24

19

My Memory Bible Verses

John 3:16-17

"For God so loved the world, that he gave his only Son, that whoever believes in him should not perish but have eternal life. For God did not send his Son into the world to condemn the world, but in order that the world might be saved through him."

Romans 6:23

"For the wages of sin is death, but the free gift of God is eternal life in Christ Jesus, our Lord."

Romans 10:13

"For everyone who calls on the name of the Lord will be saved."

Psalm 56:3

"When I am afraid, I will trust in you."

Philippians 4:13

"I can do all things through Christ who strengthens me."

Ephesians 4:32

"Be kind to one another, tenderhearted, forgiving one another, as God in Christ forgave you."

1 Peter 5:7

"Cast all your worries on him because he cares for you."

This book belongs to:

—————◆•◆—————

_____

Name

Hi! My nickname is_____.

I am _____ years old.

My birthday is on_____.

Today, _____, I accepted the

Lord Jesus Christ as my God, my Lord, and my Savior.

I love Jesus because:

_____

_____

_____

_____

_____

_____

_____

_____

My Short Bible Quiz:

1. What is the name of the notorious prisoner mentioned in the story?_____

2. How many days had passed before Jesus Christ rose from the dead?_____

3. Fill in the blank:
   "_____ awaits a man, with God in Heaven he will find!"

4. Jesus is not only your Healer, your Giver, but most importantly, he is your _____!

5. True or false:
   Jesus is your Lord, God, and Savior. _____

About the Author

Joy hails from the humble town of Arayat, Pampanga. Raised by her mother, lolos, lolas, titos, titas, and tens of relatives from her extended family, she would always find a piece of solace by sitting in one corner and rummaging through the pages of her favorite children's book.

Growing up from an unlikely place, a community behind a public cemetery, Joy would always see the "white plains" as a tiny kingdom where imaginations can turn into her unsung realities.

On sunny days, she would go playing outside, hopping on tomb after tomb, hunting for tadpoles, snails, and dragonflies. Her love for reading stories and adventure ignited her passion for writing. Joy's colorful childhood contributed a lot in how she sees life today. It is amazing how in that tiny place where most kids fear visiting, a little girl once dreamed of writing her own book someday.

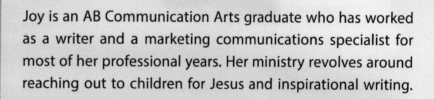

Joy is an AB Communication Arts graduate who has worked as a writer and a marketing communications specialist for most of her professional years. Her ministry revolves around reaching out to children for Jesus and inspirational writing.

She is a mother of two and enjoys her free time reading. Currently, Joy is working on writing Christian children's books as her 'monument' for the Lord Jesus Christ.

To the One who never gave up on me since day one,
my loving and graceful God, this is for You.

To Rapha and Toby, you both are God's tangible evidence of His grace to me.
I am a better woman for loving you two.

To my husband, my better half, and my God's will, RJ.
I can't thank you enough for all the support you've shown me. I love you.

To Sis. Elai, Sis. Joanna, Sis. Liza, Sis. Joy, and Sis. Meng, and Sis. April,
I praise God for using you to help me realize and embrace my true calling.

To my brothers and sisters in Christ, my Prayer Room warriors, and my loved ones,
all of you are God's instruments in molding me to be the person that I am today.

To my mom, Jolly, my heart longs for you. This book is also for you.

To the children, may you get to know, love, and seek Jesus more.
Hold on to Him until the very end.

Who Is Jesus? *is Holy Spirit-led and written for you.*

Printed in Great Britain
by Amazon